DB MacInnes
What Love Survives & Other Stories

Front cover image by Erin Garrett

The Lost Squadron

("The Lost Squadron" was first published in *Product Magazine* on 23rd December 2017 and every 23rd December since then.)

I imagine the boy heard the roar of the engine long before the aeroplane emerged from the mountains of Skye. It took shape slowly; an incarnation of wire, stretched canvas and wooden struts staying impossibly aloft. This biplane from another age finally soaring above his head, before beginning its descent towards the deserted island airstrip.

The aeroplane was recognisable of course, from boys' comics, where it looped and dived against the Hun, machine guns chattering above the shriek of the wind. High up on the hill, the boy would only just have recovered from his shock and delight, when another droning engine announced the coming of a second biplane. One after another they came quickly then, like ghosts out of the mist, as if the first had broken through some invisible membrane and made the passage of the others possible.

I picture him running down the hill to the four Sopwith Camels, lined up at the end of the airstrip and ready to scramble at a moment's notice, the pilots pulling off their helmets and goggles, as they made their solemn way across the tarmac to the hangar. Christmas Eve was the next day, but it must have felt like his gifts for all time were sitting on that tarmac, engines ticking, exhausts reeking of burnt oil, propellers still spinning in the wind.

The bare bones of this I took from the boy's diary, but most of it is my own fancy. What the diary suggests happened on that day, has taken root in my mind, and good or bad, true or untrue, it has worked its enchantment.

* * *

I am, was Christy's teacher before he vanished. I arrived a year ago on the island of Flodday, on the big ferry boat from Mallaig, which had to be met off-shore by the lugger, as there wasn't the harbour or the depth to accommodate her. It was the last run before Christmas, with a weather front closing in. The sea was already choppy, but the lugger made the run, and I was lucky to get off the ferry at all. Sometimes it just had to turn around, the island folk on the slipway watching the big boat with its passengers and cargo, disappearing back over the horizon.

Highland Council had contracted me to begin teaching at the two-room school after the Christmas holidays, but for the previous three years, the festive season had been difficult for me. I liked to go away at that time to a place I'm not known. No-one on Flodday knew me, or how Marie and I had lost Dougal, and then each other.

Christy's mum, Alison, was the first person I met, as I walked up the slipway, my kitbag held on my shoulder with one hand, and suitcase in the other. I suppose she was picking up some mail-order item from the lugger. The first thing I noticed about Alison was her smile. It began in her eyes, and then her lips stretched upwards, so generous they refused to part. That morning her dishwater blonde hair was tied back loosely with a faded blue scarf.

The day Christy disappeared she showed up at my cottage where it sits at the other end of the bay from the village. It got dark by five o'clock so I know it was late. Where I live there are no streetlights, so when I opened the door, Alison was lit only by the lamp in my hall. She had not yet stumbled on his diary, so her face was still calm.

She entered my living room and looked around. 'I guess you're not big on Christmas, Graham.' She shook her head. 'Not even a holly wreath on the door?'

I shrugged. 'There was a time I couldn't be seen for baubles and tinsel. But that time has gone.'

Alison looked keenly at me then, but said nothing.

I offered her a seat. 'What can I do for you?'

'I thought maybe Christy might be here playing chess. He hasn't come home yet and I've looked in all the usual places. I know what you two are like when you get your heads into a game.'

'We played chess on Friday, after school closed for the holidays. I haven't seen him since.'

Her face fell. 'He always comes home in time for supper. Graham, I'm beginning to worry.'

'Have you tried the airstrip? I heard a couple of planes landing this morning.'

'When he didn't show up for his tea, it was the first place I sent Jake to.'

This was surprising to me, as Jake, her most recent man, had shown little interest in the lad, or in complying with any of Alison's wishes. His handsome face seemed set in a permanent scowl. A few weeks ago, Christy had come to school with a black eye. I had asked him about it, but he just said he had tripped in the mud and fallen against the wood store outside their house.

When I set projects at school, if I didn't tightly specify them, Christy would find a way of including planes, and the more antique the better. He drew biplanes from the First World War on any scrap of paper he could find, his tongue stuck out in concentration as he traced the tricky ailerons and landing gear. The island's airstrip called to him, although it's little used. Sometimes in an emergency a patient might be flown to the mainland hospital. Occasionally Flodday's landowners, the folk in the Big House, use it to fetch friends and family from the South.

The following morning Alison was back at my door, her hair uncombed and her eyes bleary with lack of sleep. She carried a brown notebook which she handed to me.

'Graham, he's still not come home. I don't know what to do. I found his diary. I want you to read it, it doesn't make any sense to me.' She started to cry. 'All his presents are under the tree. Why isn't he here to open them?'

I sat her in an armchair while I turned over the pages of the lined notebook. Christy had written in blue ink, using the fountain pen he proudly carried to school after his dad sent it to him.

'Sopwith Camels. Fantastic. They each made a perfect landing, amazing to watch. They smell of oil and cordite. "H2001" (that's the captain's), "H2003", "H2007", "H2012"? Why are there gaps between the numbers? Behind the captain's cockpit ten holes have been shot through the fabric in a straight line. Pure dead brilliant.'

And later, scribbled in a hurry, using a pencil. 'I've had enough. This is my chance to get off the island. I've asked the Captain to take me with him.'

I wondered why, if Christy left voluntarily, he didn't take the diary. Did he hope when we read it, he might save us the bother of searching? Or did he think the words might comfort his mum? In this age of Xboxes and the Internet, the keeping of a journal by a child was unusual and perhaps too much so. I entertained the possibility of fabrication by a more mature mind, but then suppressed the thought and turned to Alison. 'This is like something out of Christy's head,' I said. ' Have you really looked everywhere?'

She nodded.

'Have you checked with Sandy the Boat?'

'There was one ferry yesterday, and Sandy managed to get out to meet it, but Christy wasn't with him.'

'He's maybe hiding somewhere.' I only said this for something to say. Snow had fallen on the previous night and the temperature was minus five.

I hesitated, and then on impulse I asked, 'How are things at home?'

Alison looked up from her hands which were twisting and untwisting a cord from her skirt.

'Not great. Jake hasn't found work since he came here and it hasn't done his temper any good.' She let go of the cord. 'But you mean Christy and Jake don't you? It's true they have never got on. But it's been no worse than usual.' She tried to smile. 'People get Jake wrong, I think.'

I looked down at the diary again. 'These numbers that Christy lists. Do they identify the planes?'

'Constable Sandilands phoned the Fort William Police and told them the numbers, and they ran some checks with the Civil Aviation folk. They didn't come up with anything.' She raised her hands helplessly. ' If these planes exist, no one can identify them.'

After she left, I called an old friend from university days. Fred is a historian, but above all he's a researcher. Without much hope, I gave him the few details I had gleaned from the diary, and asked him to let me know if anything came up.

Then I phoned Constable Sandilands, the island's only policeman, to see how I could help with any searches being planned. As I waited for him to phone back, I thought about the contents of the diary.

Something in me was already beguiled, I confess, by the story of the planes and by the mysterious 'Captain'. It's a rank that resonates more than any other, elevated just enough to command respect, but close to the action. Living amongst Gaels had unmoored me a little, from my trust in the material nature of being. As they went about their business, in the day or in the night, the locals were mindful of a parallel world whose dwellers were excited by mischief. No one was surprised when occasionally the thin veil which separated the two was torn. Christy was twelve years old. The age of admission to Neverland. Had Christy flown 'second to the right, and straight on till morning'? God knows, it would be lovely to believe that all lost boys took this path, rather than the one to oblivion.

Later that day I found myself on the hill that divides the village from the airstrip, where, if the contents of the diary were true, Christy had seen the biplanes arrive. Snow was still falling and had built up on the high ground. As we searched, we plunged our long poles into the drifts, anticipating the slight give which a body yields. In another time and another place, I had been a member of a rescue team, but that day, as time passed, I found myself uncovering more than dead bodies on that hill.

A coastguard helicopter had been buzzing around since mid-morning, but by late afternoon it had left, and Constable Sandilands had rounded up the search parties and sent them home.

Alone, tramping through the crisp snow in the last of the daylight, I allowed a wintry memory to emerge which for years I had held at bay. A small hand in mine and the crunch of feet, every few seconds running to keep up with my stride.

I suppose the effort of maintaining that wall between my waking life and the dreams in which Dougal appeared to me, had become too much, and sooner or later it was going to crumble. I stood there on the hillside as my tears fell at last, and found that I welcomed them. I realised then, that I had to make a choice. To continue to mourn or to cherish.

I made my way down the hill to the cottage, passing through a grove of young spruce trees. Some of them had been lopped off at the base by islanders taking Christmas trees, in defiance of the folk in the Big House.

The phone rang at seven o'clock on Christmas Day. I leaped from my bed, stumbling through the frosty air of the hallway, hoping because of the early hour, it would be Alison with good news. It was Fred.

He could hardly contain his excitement. 'You know I was brought up beside RAF Halton?'

'No I didn't. It's seven o'clock, Fred. For God's sake, what is it?'

'No need to be like that Graham,' he said. 'I know it's early. Anyway, they had a history museum at Halton for all the aircraft that ever passed through. So I knew right away the "H" in the registration was used by the Royal Flying Corps. That was easy. But I tell you, it was the numbers following the letter which made the hair on the back of my neck rise. I didn't say anything at the time, because I wanted to be sure.'

'The numbers didn't mean anything to the Police or to the Civil Aviation Authority.'

'No they wouldn't. If data is paper-based these characters don't want to know. Lazy buggers. I mean, how many man-hours would it take to digitise it? I've written —'

'Fred! Tell me what you've got.'

'Okay. Keep your hair on.' Fred went into the ponderous lecturing style he thought impressed his students. '"H2001" was the number of the plane flown by Captain Robert Penwaller when he took off from Heathfield RFC Station in Ayrshire, on the morning of the 23rd of December 1917.'

'Hold on,' I said, 'two days before Christmas?'

'Correct. He had three other planes with him. They were all that remained of his squadron, which had taken a severe mauling from German Fokkers in the previous week. Penwaller was waiting for the War Office to assign new pilots to the squadron, but by all accounts he was pretty gung-ho, so he volunteered for light duties out of Heathfield patrolling in the Irish Sea. That morning they had been tasked with replacing the escort of a small convoy heading into Belfast from New York. Eye-witnesses said they took off, shook themselves out into standard flying formation and flew into the mist which was beginning to gather out at sea.'

Here Fred paused for full effect.

'They were never seen again.'

He stopped speaking then and we were both quiet for a while. Eventually my mind returned from whichever realm it had wandered to.

'Exactly one hundred years ago,' I said.

'Exactly.'

'Thank you, Fred.' I replaced the receiver.

It rang again almost straight away.

'Graham, Graham, is that you?' It was Alison. 'We found him, Graham. We found him.' She was crying down the phone and laughing at the same time.

'Where?'

'He's at his dad's in Cornwall. We've been trying to track his dad down for ages, but he keeps moving and he's changed his phone and Christy never told us. Eventually we got his number from an old workmate. Then we left messages, but he wasn't checking his answerphone, the idiot.'

'It's a long way,' I said. 'How are you going to get Christy back?'

'Oh Graham.' Her voice shook. 'He says he needs some time with his dad just now. He and Jake just can't share the same space. He's getting to be a man I suppose.' There was a pause, and muffled words, as if she was speaking to someone else in the same room. Then she came back. 'His dad is going to keep him for a couple of months, while I sort things out here. I'm going to miss him so much.'

I didn't ask her how Christy had made the long journey down to Cornwall, let alone got off the island. She had her boy back, and the return of a child from Neverland, as I knew, was a gift seldom bestowed. We wished each other a happy Christmas, and she invited me round for dinner with her and Jake, which I declined.

I walked through to the kitchen and filled the kettle and placed it on the hob. A couple of pine cones lay on the floor. They had fallen from the Christmas tree I had cut down in the forest on my way home. I had decorated it with holly berries and with pine cones, tied on with scraps of red netting from a whelk sack. *Let Alison come and visit me now.*

Then I turned and leaned against the range, feeling the heat rising against my thighs, and stared out of the window. It was still night outside, the stars winking bright against the infinite dark. Under the window there was a table and on it was a framed picture of Dougal I had retrieved from the suitcase under my bed. Beside the picture sat a tangle of worn leather, steel buckles and amber coloured glass. Picked up on yesterday's walk round the airstrip, they now made me smile. They looked very much like Royal Flying Corps goggles.

The Girl From The West

("The Girl From The West" was first published in 2017 in the 34th edition of *Northwords Now* as "The Night Visitor". Editor Kenny Taylor.)

The room was above the newsagent on the promenade. It must have originally been a store. You got in through the fire-escape at the back. There was a bay window looking east over the Firth of Forth where it runs out to the North Sea. A cast iron stove sat on the lime-washed floorboards and there was a sink with a cold water tap. That was all. He could use the newsagent's toilet when it was open, but it was understood that the arrangement was not official. At night when trying to sleep, he could hear the sonorous cries of the ships' foghorns out at sea.

He was grateful for the room as he needed somewhere to bring the kids. Some months after he lost his job, his marriage also ended. As he was falling asleep one night, a thought came to him unbidden and he murmured to his wife, 'Now, when we make love it feels like you're being unfaithful to someone.' In the morning he woke to find her crying. She was having an affair with her boss who reminded her of her father.

The kids were great. On their way round to see him, they scavenged along the beach collecting driftwood for the stove. To them, Daddy seemed to be on a camping trip without end. They brought round a TV-with-video that their granny had bought for their bedroom.

By now he had found a couple of discarded pallets to form a base for a bed, and blew one week's unemployment benefit on a mattress. He and the kids sat on it wrapped in blankets and watched old Doctor Who episodes as the tiny cracks in the stove glowed red in the darkness.

From the marital home he received the chaise longue and matching chair he had refurbished in a night class, which he used to improve the look of the room, until he sold them to pay for a set of bagpipes.

A year ago, at a time when his low spirits had exhausted the sympathy of even his kindest friends, he had watched an old man in the street playing the bellows-blown pipes, the quieter kind. The old man's hat was upturned for tips, his face ardent and spry. The sound of the chanter and drones rose like the thrum of bees in summer. After the pipes were delivered, care of the newsagents downstairs, he practiced every morning before they opened and at night after they closed.

To give his days some structure he attended college, on a back-to-work scheme. Not caring what he did, he picked Computer Studies. On the first day, a girl entered the lecture room with the swagger of a young thug. She was tall with short red hair and she scanned the room as she made her way to her desk. When their eyes met, she gave him a wicked grin.

A week later they met in a queue for the bar at a student party. By the time they hit the street, he had told her about his wife, his kids and the looming divorce and then he left her at the corner so he could piss behind a wall. He was mildly surprised to come back and find her still waiting.

When they got to the room, there was no wood for the stove that wintry night. She pushed him back onto the bed, and they climbed in without having kissed. Both still drunk, their bodies folded into one another almost by accident, and a little while afterwards she got up to be sick. She left in the early hours of the morning and he lay on in happy disbelief. All that term, each time they met, he noticed their first touch relieved some previously unrecognised pain.

After lectures, they fled back to his room, guided through the evening streets by the orange blossoms of the lamps in the mist, their shoes ringing out like iron on the cold stone. For years afterwards, each time the fog rolled in from the North Sea and crept up through the city, he would think of her.

She was a former hairdresser from Paisley who had become allergic to the chemicals used in her work. Since that alteration, she had departed from the fashions of the West. What she wore now was jeans, an old pullover and converse sneakers. It was the first time he had slept with a woman who wore her femininity so lightly and who was so comfortable with silence. One day she wanted to cut his hair, which she did without a mirror, while not responding to his attempts at conversation. He wondered if he had caused offense, but in the middle of cutting she put down the scissors, placed her head against his and kissed him, then lifted the scissors again. Another time they were in bed and making love when she began to cry. He drew back in alarm and looked at her.

'It's nothing. I'm just happy' she said.

She was the kind of girl that men talked to easily. They chose not to banter with her and she did not flirt. They might talk about motor-bikes, a subject on which she was informed. They might talk about music, which she saw as a vast city, whose main thoroughfares should be avoided, while in the back-streets treasures were exchanged. The folk tunes he played were nice, but museum pieces. She thought the world had produced too many people, that time was impossible to measure, and that the planet was doomed. Sometimes after she had smoked weed, which she did often, she seemed to inhabit a separate domain and could not be reached.

When the kids came at the weekend, she stayed away. Sometimes he took them on a bus out to the hills, trying to climb a different one each time, trying for a sense that their lives were moving forward. But there was one time when they were leaving the room that he began to weep. His son turned away but his daughter was affected and wrote about it for school in a 'what I did at the weekend' report.

The next day at college he tried to talk about the kids but she changed the subject and persuaded him to skip the lecture to catch a bus back to the room. They spent the rest of the day in bed. In the evening he got up to fry bacon on the stove and they took sandwiches down to sit on the sea wall, where the moon emerged from the clouds to throw down a shining path across the water. Usually she did not stay all night, but that evening they fell asleep and did not wake until dawn. Later on she caught the bus home, and at the stop outside the flat she shared with her boyfriend, the doors opened to reveal him waiting to go to work. It seemed he passed her by without comment.

There were times when she was absent for long periods. One day when he was expecting her, she didn't show up, nor was she at college the next two days. It seemed her pal's boyfriend had been holding some crack cocaine for a dealer, and the girls thought they would try it when the boyfriend was out. They only stopped when it was finished. When the boyfriend returned and discovered the loss, he started beating her pal up, so she took the baseball bat which was kept behind the front door and knocked him out.

In her absence, he would retreat to the pipes. He hung onto each note, his fingers on the chanter feeling the vibration from the two slips of spanish cane, the resonance filling the room.

He loved especially the playing of a slow air, the melody yearning for what is lost or what cannot be. It was then the night visiting began. Even now, she comes to his dreams, the haunt continuing throughout the waking day.

In the end the absences simply got longer, until finally the course was over. They both passed and she got a distinction. She appeared on the fire-escape one Sunday morning not long after the results came through. He opened the door and as always the sight of her face made his head swim. She only wanted to make love, but on leaving she turned and looked hard at him. 'You take care of yourself. For I'll not be back.' Then she vanished through to the West forever.

It took him a long time to get over it but underneath the sadness was a feeling which grew, that she had left him with more than when they began, and surely that was the moon, the fog, the pipes and the self who remembered.

What Love Survives

("What Love Survives" was first published in *Gutter 20* (Glasgow, Gutter, 2019), edited by Colin Begg, Henry Bell, Kate MacLeary.)

Clare is favouring her right side because the wound is still painful. She shows Jack a wildflower growing by the side of the path. The two blonde heads bend over it, her left arm around his body. Jack's fully grown now, but is still ungainly and likely to trip. Today he is less agitated, and from his throat come sounds which express interest, even joy. There was a time when mother and son would have needed my strength, but this morning I might as well not be here.

Our walks from the cottage restore me in a way I never expected. It's so quiet in this place, a far-off grouse calling *gobackgobackgoback* startles me. The big skies are untroubled by the distant mountains, the mist lingers in the hollows of the land, the terrain seems so boundless, that you could imagine walking a hundred miles without meeting another human soul. Back in the city, going out with Jack wasn't easy because of cyclists and dogs and the sound of traffic. He likes his environment to be silent or grotesquely loud. Nothing in between.

I first saw Clare at a Halloween party in an Edinburgh tenement, her blonde fringe hanging over a face of queer beauty. She had left art school two years previously. I already had one marriage behind me, and I was not hopeful about love. We slept together that first night in my single bed. In the morning, we were entwined like neolithic lovers revealed by brush and trowel.

I loved only books and music then. Clare's loves were art and the natural world. Merwomen and fish swam through her landscapes of ochre and teal. That first morning when we got up, the rain was lashing at the windows of my little flat overlooking the Forth estuary. After breakfast she dragged me along Portobello beach in the teeth of the storm. Our first date was up on Salisbury Crags, that dark escarpment which looms over the city. In time, she persuaded me along the coast to where the sun lit up the pink battlements of Tantallon Castle. It seemed to me that at last someone had turned the light on in my life. But such careless love was long ago, and what love survives our path through the world?

When Jack came along, in that innocent but fleeting time when he was a baby, I would cradle him in my arms and vow to protect him. Of course nature ignored my promises. Soon, a perceptive health visitor noticed that milestones were being missed. By the time Jack was three years old, his rages were like hourly storms of protest at the blight which arrested his launch into the world. His mind is an unfinished craft, keel and frames exposed to the weather, a vessel he will never captain.

With Jack the difficulty is not just about feeding and dressing and bottom-wiping. Like everyone, he wants to be understood, and if we're slow to recognise his sounds and signs, he becomes enraged. Then he wants his favourite person in all the world to make things better and that person is Clare. He punches himself in the face, again and again, until he gets her attention. He's found what works, and like anyone else, he uses it. This is why his face always displays bruising, some old and yellow, some new and dark. Stains like those on his bedroom walls, during episodes when he rediscovers his fascination with excrement. Clare, who taught Art, was first to give up her job.

I sometimes wonder how much Jack understands. Does he fear the reefs and shoals of his passage through life? Does he compare himself to others of his age? I hope not, because I cannot bear to think that beneath his anger lies sadness, with him all his days.

What was manageable for some years became less so when the taxi which collected Jack each morning for school stopped coming. A week before his eighteenth birthday, we had a visit from his social worker, Sally Meecham. With her dark hair like a perfect helmet and in her smart green coat which she chose not to remove, she stood in our kitchen and said, 'We'll be passing the baton to Adult Services.'

To her credit she looked regretful. She knew what that meant. It was her first job since leaving college and already, like a nun in a red-light district, the knowledge of sin had entered her never to leave. By then, she realised that the miracles her college books told her she could perform needed money. There was none.

Soon after that, I resigned from my job as a teacher of English. Jack's increasing size were too much for Clare. From a care-giving charity we received one hour of respite, five days a week, during which we got outside in all weathers, although it wasn't enough. When Jack was at school, Clare had been free to draw and paint for a few hours each day, but that time had run out. Like the flowers and trees she so loves and more than anyone I know, Clare needs sunlight and wind and rain. Deprived of these, her spirits dwindle and her canvases are bare.

It didn't make sense for all of us to be trapped. I alone had the strength to restrain Jack from self-injury. When he started to punch himself, I would grip his fists from behind and pull him into me, both of us locked together until I felt his body relax. Then Clare would join us, and we would stand with our arms around each other, as one. Always, before Clare and I were quite ready, Jack would return to his remedy for all upsets; his tablet and his games.

We decided that each day after our morning walk, Clare would collect her drawing books, her paints, her charcoals and leave the house, returning later so we could both get Jack out into the fresh air. It did me good to see her skipping through the door, the golden girl I remembered, although we did not realise that in Jack some subterranean disorder had begun.

One Saturday in the park, a passer-by brushed against him, something he would usually ignore.

This time he screamed and began to punch himself in the face. Clare tried to reassure him, but Jack's arm swept round and caught the side of her head. Her knees gave way, and she fell into some bushes by the side of the path. A few people stopped to stare. I restrained Jack, assuming Clare would soon regain her feet, but instead a chilling cry rose from the bushes. I ran over. She lay there, blood bubbling around a thin spike of metal, which had pierced her side from back to front.

I looked round at the people and yelled at them to help us. Jack had realised by now that something dreadful had occurred. He was curled up in the foetal position and moaning. I reached for Clare and was about to lift her, but a man stepped forward and pinioned my arms.

'No, ye eejit', he said, 'don't ye be touching her now. We have to keep her dead still.'

The authority in his lilting Irish accent made me stop. I guessed he was a medic, but still I wailed, 'We can't leave her like this.' Clare groaned and in the background I heard someone on a phone demanding an ambulance.

The Irishman considered the spike which was from a broken shopping trolley and spoke more kindly. 'Sure now, the paramedics will have the proper tools, but we can do something.'

He produced a pocket knife, removed his shirt, then cut the sleeves off which he rolled up into makeshift pads. With one hand he dragged soil away from underneath Clare and inched a pad under her back. Then he wrapped the other around the spike in front and said, 'Press this firmly now. Be sure nothin moves.'

I did as he said, saying Clare's name over and over, an incantation of loss. Her eyes opened at last. 'Ed', she said, 'Ed. See to Jack', and her eyes slid past me to where our son lay shaking on the ground.

'I will. Don't worry', I said. 'The ambulance is coming.'

The Irishman had been speaking on a phone with some urgency, but now he handed it back to its owner and took over from me so I could be with Jack. Ten minutes later the ambulance arrived. The paramedics assessed Clare's injury and decided the spike had to remain until they got her into surgery. They dug away more earth and cut the spike with heavy, long-handled, metal snips. The Irishman put his ruined shirt back on, and I regret to this day that I forgot to thank him.

The next morning as I helped Jack to get dressed, he signed to me, tapping three fingers on his palm.

'Mum? You want to know about Mum?' I said. 'You remember what happened yesterday, Jack? Mum's in hospital, but I phoned and they said she's going to be fine. We'll visit her this afternoon. Don't worry. '

Usually, Jack's attention skips from one thing to another, but that morning his blue eyes locked on mine, and it seemed to me that in them I saw what I had dreaded; Jack's understanding of his place in the world might be greater than we imagined. How would he cope when Clare and I were no longer around? I knew then that as long as I was alive, I could not have him in a locked ward with white-coated staff impatient to get off their shift. Looking back now, it's apparent that something had become too finely balanced in my mind, and in that moment it began to tip.

On the following Monday, Jack and I planned a visit to Clare in the afternoon. During morning respite, I abandoned the beach and the local park, drove out to South Queensferry and strolled a little way onto the Forth Road Bridge. From the footway I gazed down at the swirling river, and into my mind came a vision of a macabre baptism, the water closing over two heads. Horrified, I broke out of my reverie. Jack hated cold water. So did I.

On Tuesday, I found myself at South Gyle train station. I walked onto the platform, found a bench, sat on it and waited. Fifteen minutes later, the train from Dunblane shot through, not stopping, rushing past with a ghastly clatter, disturbing the very air on the platform with the shock of its passing. Jack loved trains. The phantasm which came unbidden to my mind then was monstrous, no less so because it was compounded by a vision of Clare painting in her studio, quite alone. I stood up and walked quickly out of the station.

The spike had missed Clare's vital organs, but some additional surgery was required, so an operation was scheduled for Wednesday morning. We wouldn't go to the hospital that day because she would be sleeping in the afternoon. After lunch, which was pizza, Jack's favourite, I announced, 'We're going to watch the trains this afternoon, Jack. What do you think of that?'

He nodded his head with excitement. I had just gone into the hallway to get our coats when there was a knock at the front door. I opened it and there stood Sally Meecham. She looked older, less well-groomed, her hair escaping from under a knitted hat.

'I heard about Clare', she said. 'I'm so sorry. But I might have some good news.'

I hesitated, in two minds.

'Let me come in Ed', she said softly.

In the kitchen, as I listened to her, Sally's eyes seemed to scan me in a considering way that wouldn't have happened two years ago. Despite Jack no longer being her case, in her off-duty time Sally had discovered another charity. They operated from Inverness and were called Highland Respite. They owned a cottage near Glenmoriston which they allocated on a weekly basis to carers. However, the best thing about their offer was this. The person cared for would be looked after in their own home, by Highland Respite workers, while the caregivers got a break.

'I thought', said Sally, 'it would help with Clare's recuperation?'

The images conjured up by her offer swept away the black thoughts of that morning. A cottage, a place to breathe, surrounded by forests, mountains and streams. Clare would sketch every day while nearby I nodded over a book. For a week everything would stop. I stumbled out some words of thanks.

At the front door, Sally said, 'Ed, when you come back, I can get you help.' She reached out and laid her hand on my shoulder and in that second the dammed-up part of me built up over the years almost gave way.

That afternoon I took Jack to Dalmeny Station where we stood on a footbridge and watched as a train thundered towards us from the cantilevered red maw of the Forth Railway bridge. As it passed below, Jack beat the iron gridwork of the railings in ecstasy while I welcomed the mechanical roar which obliterated my thoughts.

In her hospital bed, Clare gripped my hand and smiled at the news. The week available to us was in a month's time, so after she came home, every night we explored the Glenmoriston area on the Internet, planning our first week alone together since Jack's birth.

Two days before our trip, we received an email from the charity. They were deeply apologetic. The support workers allocated were no longer available. One had just resigned to look after her mother who had been diagnosed with a terminal illness. The other had emailed Highland Respite from Thailand. He had gone on a fortnight's leave and decided to keep travelling. Unfortunately schedules were so tight that no backup staff could be found. We could still come for the week but without support.

We ate our breakfast in silence and then Clare, tight-lipped, grabbed her drawing materials and left the house. Jack whimpered when the door slammed and sat beside me on the couch. He just wanted to be held, so I lay back, with my arms around him, listening to the traffic outside, a neighbour calling to someone in the street.

Clare returned at her usual time, but now with a wide-lipped grin I hadn't seen for a while.

'I went up on the Pentland hills', she said, 'I couldn't see much because of the clouds but I kept working.' She stared at me. 'I was ready to give up. Throw everything away.'

Then she took my hands in hers. 'Ed, the clouds parted and the sun lit up my sketchpad. I looked down and I'd made good choices after all. The colours were right, the marks were honest and I thought, we'll all go, it'll be great, we'll make it work.'

It helped that we took the train. Jack's nose was pressed to the window for most of the journey. The first morning I slept in. Clare and I had drifted into sleeping apart over the years, and had not yet resolved that difficulty. Jack rises early, and I usually get up when the chime from his bedroom warns me, but the cottage wasn't equipped for that. When I looked at my watch it was nine. In Edinburgh, more than once I'd been too slow, and Jack already had all the hob burners and the oven lit. I panicked and ran through to the cottage kitchen. Empty. Then I checked Jack's bedroom. That too was empty. Was he outside, perhaps wandering into the path of some farmer driving his tractor, in a universe where all young men had road sense? Still in my bare feet, I ran through the hallway and stopped dead on the doorstep.

There, sitting on the low drystone wall of the garden was Jack. No tablet, no headphones, just my son in the morning light, gazing towards the far-off mountains which were garlanded in mist. I walked up to the wall and sat on it, a few feet from him, then swung my legs over, so I was facing the same way. We stayed like that for half an hour, as the mist burned away from the land.

I didn't speak and Jack didn't look at me, except when Clare called us to breakfast. I turned and caught his eye and he smiled. Once again I caught that glimmer of understanding which only a few weeks ago had caused me to despair but now gave me hope. I slid off the wall and then helped Jack round to the gate. As we moved towards Clare, I saw in her eyes a question which only time will answer.

The weather in the highlands isn't always great, so on a couple of mornings we stayed indoors, and we had the usual behaviours from Jack; food thrown and refusal to dress. But all the other days of that magical week began like that first morning, blessed with cooperation and a shared contentment.

A day like today. Unlike anything we could have dreamed of before we sold the house in Edinburgh. Further down the path, Clare has paused to rest on a gate and looks up to give me that smile I love, before turning back to our son. Jack is pointing out the skull of a deer some wag has placed on a fence post, the voids of its sightless eyes framing purple heather and blue sky.

Night On The Moor

("Night On The Moor" was first published in *Product Magazine* on 10th May 2019.)

Archie was tired of listening to his mother. He shoveled porridge into his mouth at the kitchen table of their decaying house, and stared out of the door which lay open to the croftlands and beyond them to the sea. In the distance, their only cow, *Breasag*, raised her head and seemed to look at him with reproach before continuing to graze. From the garden came the sound of his sister Dolac beating life back into their threadbare carpet.

'Yon Peter MacDonald has done very well for himself,' his mother said.

'How so?'

'Well, called the Dummy all his life, but he did well in the end. Yon deaf school in Edinburgh got him speaking as well as you or me, and in two weeks he's away to the university to study medicine.'

Archie's mind drifted to tonight's ceilidh dance in the village hall and he wondered if Maggie Morrison would come. She had finished with him months ago, but he still hoped she might change her mind. Maggie, like Peter, was away to college at the end of the summer, taking away her red-gold hair and her wide-lipped smile. He pushed away his porridge bowl. 'How will he mend the sick when he can't hear them?'

'Och Archie, Archie, ' his mother replied, turning away from him, her voice fading in that way the Minister had, of dropping off to a whisper when listing the failings of his congregation.

It was his mother's birthday and he had not yet given her a gift. Shona, the younger of his two sisters, had bought their mother a new mirror from a mail-order catalogue, and he watched as she hung it above the fireplace where it would reflect and multiply the flames out into the room.

Dolac called from the garden. 'Archie, come out here and help me beat this carpet.'

He got up and behind him the chair slammed to the stone floor. His boots stood in the hallway and he stamped his feet into them. Then he was out the door, his large frame barrelling past his angry sister and on through the gate.

He turned onto the road which ran at the back of the croft houses. Constructed by gangs of redcoat soldiers two hundred years ago to promote the rule of law in the rebellious north, it was only good for offroad vehicles. He followed it along the coast before it swung away inland, over the moor. Soon he reached the High Loch, where the boys went fishing after brown trout. A dinghy was pulled up on the shore.

Just beyond the halfway stone on the redcoat road, was the sheep fank where shearing took place. Its drystone walls lay in a patch of green, cropped out of the nut brown moor over the years by the sheep. Archie abruptly left the road and leapt onto the nearest wall. These days the fank's tool store had turned into an informal club for the idle, and he hoped a few of the older men might be inside, warming themselves at the stove, but there was no smoke rising from the lum sticking through the roof.

One of the men had a prawn boat, and sometimes took Archie as crew. This was when he was happiest, pulling up creels from the green depths of the sea, their blue translucent populations all beady eyes and spidery legs.

He ran his hands over the rough stone of the wall. A memory came of his father lifting him onto it when he was a child, the khaki jacket his father always wore reeking of tobacco mixed with peat-smoke. It was a relic from his father's days in the Cameron Highlanders, fighting in the desert sands of Africa, through the olive groves of Sicily and finally on the drive for Berlin. Archie had searched in vain for that torn and faded jacket, and he mourned its loss still.

After the war his father had worked on the roads for the Highland Council, until one year without explanation, there was no work to be done. He was no fisherman, couldn't even swim, but there was nothing else for it but to sign onto Angus MacDonald's boat. Angus, who was The Dummy's father, was not famous for his attention to safety and found it difficult to acquire crew.

Sat in a corner of the sheep-fank tool shed, Archie had once overheard older fishermen talking to his father about being swept into the sea. Twenty minutes, they said. Twenty minutes before you begin to die of hypothermia. Just dive to the bottom while you still can, they said. Get it over with.

A year ago on a March day when the sea and sky were the colour of slate, a mighty wind came howling out of the north, and Angus MacDonald's boat was lost with all hands. Archie often wondered if his father, the novice fisherman, the war hero returned to navvy on council tarmacadam, finding himself tossed in the grey caverns of the ocean, remembered that bleak advice, and saying goodbye, goodbye, goodbye to his loved ones, slowly turned and slipped to the ocean's bed.

It was at this time Maggie Morrison came into Archie's life, showing him sympathy during the first few days as the dimming of hope began for the boat's return. He had clung to her as a drowning man grips a floating spar. He remembered the sudden beauty of her body as they lay in a hollow on the moor, her creamy skin pinkening and vibrating beneath his touch as he lay in a kind of rapture with her. But for Maggie it was only an act of kindness and a girl's curiosity quickly satisfied. To her, the wide world was already beckoning.

Archie dropped from the sheep fank wall, feeling the money in his pocket jingle. He had been saving to buy his mother some perfume, but a more pressing need was a bottle of whisky for the dance.

***

At the ceilidh that night Archie sat in the corner of the hall as the dancers whirled past.

The visiting band from Acharacle were playing in a fast but strict tempo. Lightest on his feet was Peter MacDonald, his body following the vibrations of the music. He and his dancing partner, a bewitching redhead with a radiant smile, were so attuned to each other that during a *schottische* they stepped and polka-ed without touching. The redhead of course, was Maggie. At one point during a barn dance she winked at Peter and threw in some extra steps as they moved apart. Next time round, he successfully copied her and she laughed.

Archie, awash with misery, stumbled back and forth to the toilets, where the men gathered with their bottles in defiance of the hall's teetotal rule. Each time he would take a long swallow from his bottle, before returning. Once he found a band follower from Acharacle in his seat, and hard words were exchanged. He nodded to the door and the lad followed him. A few minutes later Archie staggered back alone, his fists skinned and bloody.

Maggie and Peter were still entwined when the accordion faded out on the last waltz. They strolled hand in hand to the door where Maggie's father waited. Archie jerked to his feet and joined the crowd pouring out into the spring night. Maggie and her father were heading along the village street in one direction, and in the other, Peter MacDonald followed the redcoat road up to the moorlands, a solitary figure under the great tent of the stars. Archie took another swig from his bottle and lurched after him.

***

He woke at dawn to the bitter screams of the seagulls on land raids from their watery kingdoms. His clothes were soaking where he lay on the shore of the High Loch beside the dinghy. He shook his head, trying to clear a way through the alcoholic murk. *Where did Peter go last night?* A rock, stained crimson, lay beside his outstretched hand. He cudgeled away dark thoughts. *Only red lichen.*

He looked at the dinghy. It had moved from its position yesterday. He seemed to remember it rocking in the water as a heavy weight tipped from the gunwale. But his head was a sea of images, and he couldn't be sure. He got to his feet and looked around. A thick mantle of early morning mist still obscured the loch, hiding whatever stories it had to tell.

He had an urgent feeling that if only he was back in his mother's kitchen listening to her soft voice, things would be normal again. He began to walk home.

'GoBack! GoBack! GoBack!' A grouse rose before him, shrieking its alarm before sweeping away over the heather. He felt sick, but wanting to distance himself from the loch, he kept going.

In half an hour, the croft houses became visible through the mist. When he could properly see his family home he began to feel less anxious. Then he saw that a vehicle was parked in front of the house. He strained to identify it. It was a Land Rover. A white background, blue patches alternating with yellow. A Police Land Rover.

His first instinct was to run, but some admonition rose within to give him strength. In the years to come he realised fate had given him a crossroads, and he chose to meet whatever waited for him in his mother's house. At the front door, he could hear a hum of voices within, but these were arrested as he entered. His mother's living room was full of friends and neighbours, all silent, all in shock at the sight of him. Two uniforms began to rise in the corner of the room by the fire, and looking up, he caught a glimpse of his face in his sister's new mirror. *Was that blood on his cheek, or was it firelight?*

'Archie, we thought ye had wandered and got stuck in the bog,' cried his mother, rushing over to hug him. 'When ye didn't come home last night, I phoned the police. They were just about to start looking for ye.'

Then, over the top of her head, he saw another fatherless son emerging from the kitchen with a tray of tea and biscuits, another boy who had awaited a boat that would never return. Archie gently set his mother to one side and crossed the room. He took the tray from the lad, laid it on a table and threw his arms around the startled Peter MacDonald.

The Sawmillers

("The Sawmillers" was first published in *Break in Case of Silence: New Writing Scotland 39* (ASLS, 2021), edited by Rachelle Atalla and Marjorie Lotfi.)

For years I ran the images in my head like some flickering newsreel. Daddo watching his hand spinning away in apparent slow motion and the yells of the other men sounding far off as if from the forest, although one of them must have hit the power button so the huge circular saw began its last few revolutions, the whirling steel now streaked with blood.

Nana was a good storyteller. She didn't skimp on the details of what led up to the accident. All that morning, the trees felled the previous day were hitched up by Daddo and his men to the two Clydesdales who then hauled them from the forest. The big saw on its conveyer belt paid no respect to the massive trunks, ripping through the heartwood as easily as the bark and sap, slicing them into planks to be hoisted onto the tall stacks beside the cutting shed. But then, as the final plank fell away on the last of the trunks, the saw came to an abrupt halt, snagged by a stray branch which stubbornly refused to snap.

Daddo always said it didn't seem worth a thought, to lean over the conveyer belt and twitch the offending branch away. But the law of force is implacable. The saw was still on full power and held the branch in its teeth at an angle. On release the branch was propelled away from him, taking the hand that gripped it across the saw's path.

When Daddo came to his senses in the back of the car driven by one of the men, Nana was beside him, twisting a rod through the tourniquet with one hand and with the other feeding him whisky. He must have understood immediately how much his life would change. A one-handed sawmilling contractor was not going to inspire confidence among the forest-owning gentry and the hiring of an extra man in the cutting shed would cripple his profit.

It was Daddo's right hand. I know this because I used to watch him changing gear with his left, the stump with the steel hook resting on the steering wheel of the Austin A40 during the long road trips we took visiting relatives across the land; a hill farmer in Angus, a shepherd and his wife in Perthshire. He and Nana would break the journey at favoured inns, leaving Ross and me in the back seat with crisps and pop while they took a dram within. Although Ross was barely one year older than me, he got the first choice of crisp flavours because, as he often reminded me, he was my uncle.

I spent my school holidays at the sawmill which was a half-day's bus ride from Glasgow where I lived with my mother. She had the sharp looks of the dark Celts and was a lover of parties and smart clothes. My mother would press five shillings in the hand of the driver of the bus which took me to Inveraray town square a few miles from my grandparents' cabin in the forest. After the first couple of trips I considered myself a seasoned traveller and thought the money wasted.

We got on well, my mother and I, although truthfully she was more like a flatmate; one who didn't mind sharing her library books. My father preferred army life and overseas postings to confinement with our little family in a tenement flat. The kitchen with its black coal-fired range also had an alcove with a small bed. From there I looked at the window which framed the stars in the night sky. Shining, immutable, steadfast, they were a kind of comfort on nights my mother didn't come home.

Alone in the flat, I trained myself to sleep with one hand over my heart and one over my mouth. I reasoned that if an intruder tried to stab me, the prick of the knife on my hand would give me warning. Equally, anyone trying to drop poison into my mouth would have to pull my other hand away first. I've always been good each morning since then, greeting its potential with the eagerness of a survivor, and that impulse forward from hurt or doubt has remained my stratagem in life. But even now, an old man, I awake in the night with my fingers against my lips.

I didn't meet Daddo and Nana and Ross until I was eight years old because of some rift in our relationship with them, some damage which appeared to have been mended. The forest where my grandparents had contracted to cut timber was on the Inveraray Castle lands in Argyle. They arrived just after the war, in the lorries carrying their prefabricated cabins and saw gear. My Nana loved their itinerant life, and I can see her now sitting beside Daddo in the lorry, her eyes glittering with excitement.

Nana usually met me at the terminus. As the bus came to a halt, I would look in the crowd on the pavement for her feathered hat and below it her smiling face. She loved poetry written in broad Scots, my Nana, and loved to recite it. The first time I climbed down from the bus she crouched and hugged me and then, sitting back on her heels she declared,

"There's a road to a far-aff land, an' the land is yonder

Whaur a' men's hopes are set;

We dinna ken foo lang we maun hae to wander,

But we'll a' win to it yet" *

The reason I remember these verses is because I have them in her hand-writing, framed above my desk, on a card sent to me when it became clear we would never meet again.

The sawmill and the cabins in which my grandparents and their workers lived, lay in a curl of the broad river which Ross and I listened to in our beds, the currents brawling with the rocks in their path as they rushed to complete the last few miles to the sea. Half a century has passed, but if I close my eyes I can still hear that river, and smell the sharpness of newly milled timber, the woodsmoke from the stove and

Daddo's sour sweat as he entered the lean-to kitchen tacked on to the cabin. The first time I met him, Daddo lifted my hand with his hook, inspected it and said, 'Play the piano, do ye?'

Later on I secretly studied Ross's hands. He was already doing unskilled work around the sawmill and they were chapped, brown with ingrained dirt and exposure to the weather.

The main room in the cabin had a stove in one corner. Packed with timber off-cuts, it glowed red hot behind the steel guard. The bedroom doors were at each end of the room. On one wall hung the galvanised tin bath we used once a week. Ross and I played Cowboys and Indians around and on top of the timber stacks by day. At night we listened to Marty Robbins' "Gunfighter Ballads" on the wind-up gramophone, our real leather cowboy holsters and cap-guns hanging at the end of the bed.

Sometimes there were parties, a couple of people from the town, some folk from the other cabins. I remember a pair of young girls two-stepping to some accordion dance band on the radio, the stove lighting up the smiling faces around the room, as a bottle of whisky was passed from hand to hand. Always, the night finished with Daddo marching up and down, a broom doubling as a rifle held over his shoulder by his stumpy arm and hook, and he singing,

"Behold, I am a soldier bold, I'm only twenty-five years old

A finer warrior ne'er was seen from Inverness to Gretna Green" **

The cabins had water from the river, heat from the stove and light from paraffin lamps. The transistor radio I brought from Glasgow was an icon of modernity. Outside there was a privy built over a pit. Behind the privy door there was a seat with a lid, a pile of old newspapers and a bucket of sawdust to throw down the hole. There was something else in there too, a thing of wonder, but perhaps it was only a trick of light that one time, because no one else ever mentioned it.

I had woken up early one winter's morning with an urgent need. I looked out of the window at the snow on the ground and could see frost glinting on the grey boards of the privy. In my duffle coat and rubber boots, I noticed the porch door was already unlatched, but gave it no thought.

As I sat in the privy, which was so dark I had to feel for the newspaper, the early morning sun must have hit the boarding outside. A needle of light stabbed through a tiny pinhole in the larch and illuminated the wall opposite with an inverted scene. I could see the cabins and the track which wound through them towards the hazy outlines of the sawmill and timber stacks. Too young to understand the science of the camera obscura effect, it seemed to me I was witnessing a miracle, for at that time I still believed in God.

Then I heard a lorry coming up the track. I turned my head upside down, trying to see more clearly. The lorry was pulling a load of milled timber. It stopped opposite our cabin and Daddo jumped out. Some words were exchanged and then a hand appeared from the lorry window holding a roll of banknotes which Daddo took. I scrunched up my eyes, peering at the image. The lorry had none of the dark red markings of those belonging to the estate which arrived late each Friday afternoon to fetch the week's timber. It seemed to me then that it was very important to be quiet. Daddo rapped on the side of the lorry with his hook and it drove off. I waited while he entered the cabin and then I waited another five minutes, but by then it was getting cold.

Inside the cabin, I found Daddo had not gone back to bed, but was crouched rekindling the stove. He heard me enter and looked over his shoulder and seemed about to speak, but I rushed past him into the bedroom. I hadn't yet learned how to deliver a reassuring lie, but I knew enough to sense the wave of suspicion on which I closed the door.

The next time I came to visit, Nana wasn't in the town square to meet me. Later on, it was explained as a misunderstanding over the wires stretching from a telephone box in deep Argyle to our Glasgow flat. But here was a challenge to my independence. I got off the bus quickly and gave one last dutiful look around for Nana. Then I lifted my suitcase and headed out of town. Soon I was on the stony track which climbed into the hills on whose lower slopes the forest began. As I walked I imagined the welcome at the cabin which would be my reward.

In the past, snug in the green leather passenger seat of the Austin with Nana driving and talking all the while, the journey had seemed to take perhaps ten or fifteen minutes. I remembered there was a turning off the main track to the right which descended into the forest, the trees immediately closing over our heads, the passageway feeling almost subterranean, on either side the soft green light dissolving into the dark.

So when an exit to the right offered itself, I took it. After walking for another half hour, the track became overgrown and rocky and it was clear no car had ever driven down it. Although it was late afternoon, in the depths of the forest it might as well have been night. Retracing your steps is not a simple matter where there are trees. Tracks which seem like junctions on the way in, can fork away from you on the way out. An hour later so little light remained, I could barely see the trees which surrounded me. I felt my way to a huge oak and placed my back against it, then slid down to sit on my suitcase. There was nothing for it but to wait until morning, listening in the darkness to the sounds from the forest of things that don't sleep. It was December and it began to snow, the smaller flakes dodging past branches and settling on the ground. Now I had stopped walking, I began to feel cold, but it was cold unlike any I had known before.

The radio that winter had for a week recounted the story of a party of walkers benighted in a snowstorm on Rannoch Moor and except for one, all dead by morning. I wondered what it would be like to die of cold. I thought perhaps I should try calling for help. My mouth opened but the words came out as a scream which frightened me even more. For better or for worse, that night I learned the importance in life of a tight seal against such leakage.

I must have drifted into sleep, because I awoke to someone shaking me by the shoulder. At first all I could see in the darkness was a flaring torch held above the stranger's head. It was like something from my picture-book about Robin Hood. The man, dressed in clothes of browns and greens, with a piece of string holding his coat together, and a leather cap on his head, did not speak, but jerked his head upwards. I got to my feet and he lifted my suitcase, taking a few steps before he turned and beckoned me to follow. We left all the visible tracks and plunged deeper into the trees. This was a time before children were taught to distrust all strangers, and it was a time when I, perhaps more than most, still believed in their kindness.

To my surprise it took only a few minutes before we arrived at a clearing in which stood a hooped structure made of branches and covered with tarpaulin. Smoke escaped from a narrow chimney made of iron which stuck out through the roof and this led to a small makeshift stove I spotted as soon as I ducked inside. I stumbled towards it holding out my hands and fell to my knees, letting the warmth seep into every part of me.

'Thank you', I said to the stranger, who had untied his coat and thrown it in the corner of the room. He did not reply but dipped a small blackened kettle in a bucket of water by the stove and then placed it on top. Soon I was cradling a mug of cocoa. The stranger seemed to not want to speak. Instead he placed a half-finished packet of digestive biscuits within my reach, and draped a blanket around my shoulders. Then he lay down on the only bed and was quickly asleep. I sat on beside the stove until my head began to nod and then I curled up on the floor of beaten earth with the blanket over me, as usual with one hand over my mouth and one over my heart.

I awoke in the morning to the smell of oats being cooked. The man gave the pot a last stir and then dumped porridge and milk in a metal bowl and gave it to me. After breakfast he put on his coat, tied it again with string and led the way out of the shelter. Half an hour later we emerged from the trees above the sawmill. Looking back now, it was a mystery that he knew where to take me, because I hadn't told him who I belonged to. I was so relieved to see my grandparents' cabin that I took a couple of steps before turning to thank the man, but already he had disappeared into the trees.

It was early, so all were still sleeping when I knocked on the door of the cabin. Daddo let me in but said nothing, instead calling to Nana and Ross. When we were all assembled in the main room he barked, 'Where the hell have ye been?'

I was taken aback, particularly because Nana remained silent, but I told my story. When I came to the end, Daddo snorted. 'A fine tale. What have ye really been up to?'

I didn't know what to say. I looked at Nana who now came forward and put her arm around my shoulders. 'I thought you were coming on the late bus laddie. I'm sorry.' There was something in her voice I hadn't heard before. 'That man. He's the Dummy who used to stay in these woods in the autumn months. Couldna' hear or speak. A tinker. He stayed in a gellie like the one you describe. But lad, he's been dead ten years. He mended our pots once, but died soon after.'

'The boy's a liar, that's what he is,' said Daddo. He turned to Nana. 'I'll bet some of these estate keepers found him and he's been blabbing...'

'Och Daddo, don't say that about the lad,' said Nana. Her voice trailed off. 'Maybe the Dummy came back..?'

'Oh aye, back from the dead, right enough Lizzie.' He looked me up and down. ' Could be the boy's just like his mother.'

Things were never the same after that morning. Ross and I went to look for the tinker's gellie but I wasn't much help; one clearing looked much like another. When Nana put me on the bus at the end of the week, from her lips came no poetry. She paid the bus-driver and then handed me a paper bag with the currant buns I loved which she had made that morning.

'Ach laddie,' she said. 'Keep yer heid in they books and I see ye goin' far.' She tousled my hair, planted a kiss on my cheek, and then she was gone.

Not long after that my father returned from overseas and reviewed our domestic arrangements. A consequence of this for me was that I was sent to a military boarding school for the sons of servicemen. I never saw Ross again, but shortly before I departed for the school I eavesdropped on a drunken argument between my father and mother, and something about Ross was revealed. I had been labelled a liar, but as is often the case, it was the children who were lied to. Ross was not my uncle after all, his mother was not Nana, and his father was an American sailor my mother met on a brief visit to Tarbert. We were half-brothers.

One day near to Christmas, a time when normally I would be placed on the Inveraray bus, I received a letter from my mother. I took it with me to a room high up in one of the faux gothic towers which stood at each corner of the school. I spread the letter on a desk I favoured because above it was a window which looked west across the barrack square to the hills and forests of Argyll.

My mother wrote that my grandparents' sawmill had been broken up, the men paid off and the lorries and cabins sold. They had moved to the city of Perth to work for a timber contractor, where Nana's quick mind was useful in the office, and driving a fork-lift in the warehouse was easy enough for a man with a hook. There was something else in the envelope.

I shook it and a card dropped out from Nana with that verse I have kept with me all my days.

A year ago, I took the bus to Inveraray again, something I had promised myself I would do, until work, marriage and children got in the way. The children were grown up and by then the marriage was over, so there were no more excuses. By early afternoon I walked out of the town on the old track, now covered in tarmac. Taking the correct turning this time, I paused when the track began to descend to the river. It wasn't quite visible, but I knew it was there, because I could hear it, and now and then the sunlight reflected off the dark water curving under the foliage. Fifty years had passed and naturally the forest had seeded many children. These had won back the land on which Ross and I had played and Daddo had milled timber. Nothing could be seen now but trees.

* Violet Jacob "Craigo Woods" (1915)
** Alexander Crawford "Jock McGraw of the Forty-twa'" (1877)

Wee Tam and Roy Rogers

("Wee Tam and Roy Rodgers" was first published in 2020 in the 40th edition of *Northwords Now*. Editor Kenny Taylor.)

'Did ye ken Roy Rogers took ma daughter?' said Wee Tam. With a flick of the wrist he sent a metal beer keg spinning across the brewery courtyard.

'Oh, is that right?' I said, catching the keg from which steam still rose. Straight-armed and with a roll of my shoulders I swung it onto the gleaming stack behind me and tried to ignore Wee Tam's frown at my tone. I couldn't help it. Each morning he made the same complaint about the film cowboy from the Fifties. By evening, his mind had been wiped clean by the dregs he shook into the pint glasses that were filling above the steam machine.

All that summer I'd been working in Campbell, Hope and King's, the oldest brewery in Edinburgh. I'd failed my university exams so I wasn't going back. It was a watershed in my life. My maiden aunt had become my guardian after my parents had died in a skiing accident when celebrating their tenth wedding anniversary. A lecturer in History at Aberdeen University, she had made it clear her interest in me, and her continued support for me, was based on my academic success. I'd worked hard at retaining her affection throughout childhood, surviving all the angsty tests since then, but my lack of commitment had been exposed at last. The shock I felt was in proportion to the fear I'd accumulated over the years. After seeing the results on the noticeboard, that night I wandered from one pub to another, their windows splashing gaudy light on the pavement, their doors an invitation to oblivion.

Some of the pubs were in the Cowgate, that sunken canyon which threads its way through the Old Town and past the cobbled slopes of the brewery. Near my flat was one where musicians gathered to play jigs and reels and sing a few songs. The music was jaunty, carefree, and I especially liked when an old man turned up with a baroque flute. The bark and fat tones from the ebony cylinder made me want to dance. Later in the night more wistful airs were played, and in the first epiphany of that summer, it struck me that beyond Hip-hop, Rap or Pop, beyond even the refined output of the Conservatoires, here was beautiful music played by ordinary people.

One night I sat in my usual corner, pint in hand, drifting on the river of melody, when I noticed the old man was playing a new flute, the same dark wood, but with extra silver keys. The old one rested on the table in front of him. Propped over it was a 'for sale' sign. I swallowed my beer and fished in my pockets for change. Money was becoming a problem, but I couldn't face going back to my flat just yet, so I ordered another drink.

By the following week I'd grown so desperate for a job, I turned up at the brewery with my lunch-box under my arm. The foreman shook his head. 'Good try, son, but we don't take on students.'

Nearby, a tiny skelf of a man had just punched his card in the clock and now was doubled over laughing, his scrawny arm stretched out, finger pointing at the lunch box.

'Whit a brass neck,' he said, 'Ach, I'll take him. Since we got they Belhaven pubs, I cannae keep up.' That was Wee Tam, whose wishes held a mysterious sway throughout the brewery.

Drink was strengthening its grip on me and now I could afford it. The brewery issued a pint of export strength 'stagger' each lunchtime which made the afternoon fly, but by five o'clock there was a thirst for more and that was when the pubs opened. One night I wandered down into the Cowgate in a mood of exploration. Two men staggered from the doors of the first pub I came to. One was middle-aged, with the dusty flat cap and overalls of a plasterer, the other younger and smarter, perhaps an office worker or bank clerk. Both were drunk. Out on the street the young man fell down and with difficulty was helped up by the other, who in turn fell down, his cap falling from his head. The ruinous choreography went on and on, until I couldn't take any more. I whirled round and headed back the way I came. Later, I thought about what I had seen. *These men are hardened drinkers. Been at it for years,* I told myself.

One day I went to the canteen porter as usual for my pint of 'stagger', but got a shake of the head. I said 'What's going on?'

The man just shrugged his shoulders and nodded towards the courtyard where Wee Tam could be seen quaffing his pint, his head thrown back, his scraggy neck muscles working hard.

Later, in the afternoon, I queued in the brewery office for my wage packet. These were handed out by a pretty girl with long red hair. Her coarse banter with the other workers contrasted with her fine-boned looks. But when I stepped up, I wondered if the packet contained my final wages because she grew quiet and handed it over with an expression of sadness. Perhaps I had offended Wee Tam irreversibly? Then she winked. *So that's what I look like,* I thought. I walked away holding my wage packet and grinning like a fool.

What was in Wee Tam's head, I would never find out, but that night I realised that it was the first time I'd been properly sober for weeks. I climbed the winding stairs to my flat, cooked a nourishing meal and considered the rich flavours of this new life. Later on I lifted the wooden flute I'd bought from the old man in the pub with my first wages. With only one term of recorder lessons at school, it took me two weeks to get a serviceable embouchure. A month later I had a set of jigs.

As the summer continued, I noticed that in good weather the red-haired girl took her lunch down into the courtyard to sit on one of the barrels where the sun was strongest. One afternoon I strolled over with my lunch-box, and mustering a smile which I hoped did not show my desperation, I sat down.

'Ye're no fuckin' shy,' she said.

I couldn't think of what to say. Then, by some divine intervention I discovered the fear inside me had a tap and by some strange alchemy it was possible for me to turn it. 'I'm shy with everyone else,' I said. 'You must bring out the best in me.'

She was drinking from her bottle of lemonade and her laughter made the fizzy liquid go down the wrong way. On clearing her nose and mouth and wiping her eyes, she looked me up and down. 'There's more to ye than fuckin' meets the eye, posh boy.'

Our sly teasing continued each time we met. It seemed like an act of intimacy that we shared our lunch-boxes; she was intrigued by my tuna and cucumber sandwiches, I craved the caramel wafers which her mother seemed to tip into her box by the half dozen. One day, we had traded happily again when I said, 'Wee Tam and Roy Rogers, eh?'

'What d'ye mean?'

'Well, all this stuff about Roy Rogers taking his daughter?'

She frowned. 'Aye, what about it?'

'Was he riding Trigger at the time?' I laughed at my joke, but she didn't join in.

'It's true,' she said.

'Really?'

'Aye, it was in the papers. My mum told me. The cowboy and his missus visited Edinburgh, went to the orphanage and fell for her.'

'Wow. She was in an orphanage?' I was rattled by this and said the first thing to come into my head. 'With Wee Tam's drinking, I guess he couldn't make a fuss.'

She stared at me. It was clear I had misstepped. 'That's where you're fuckin' wrong. Wee Tam stopped drinkin' when his wife fell ill with cancer. Nursed her for a year he did, but the girl was taken into care as it was gettin' too much for him. But it was only meant to be a few weeks.'

I felt miserable, for Wee Tam, for the blighted family, for myself. But her look softened and also her voice. 'Then Roy Rogers came to town. Aye and his missus and Trigger too. Rode Trigger up the steps of the Council Assembly Rooms he did. After they visited the orphanage, the Social came round to Wee Tam and they gave him the choice. What I heard was he went up on the Pentland Hills all day and when he came back down, his mind was made up. What was best for the lassie.'

'Christ, what a choice to make,' I said.

'Aye, but a good one for her. They took her over to their ranch in Montana and brought her up with their other kids.'

'And what about Wee Tam?'

She made a fist and punched my arm. 'The day she left, he started drinkin' again.'

So the next morning I got to work in plenty of time. As usual Wee Tam sent the kegs spinning crazily over the cobbles, the sun flashing off their metal bodies. I had to be quick to catch them before they crashed into my knees. Nevertheless when Wee Tam finally said, 'D'ye ken Roy Rogers took ma daughter?', I was ready.

'Aye Tam, I know, and I'm sorry,' I said. ' D'ye want to talk about it?'

Of all the things I learned on the streets of Edinburgh that summer, the one from Wee Tam was the best. A lesson got without the goading of fear, from a small man with a big heart. The thing that drives us is love. The all-consuming power of love.

The Boy Who Vanished

Yesterday was All Souls' Day in Achnabeg. That time of the year when we remember the poor souls in purgatory, as the hours of daylight squeeze through the mist and fog and get lost again in the night. Ach, it's then we usually look forward with hope to the good cheer of Christmas and Hogmanay, but this year is different. Angus Dubh and John-Norman were washed up on the shores of Staffin Island over by Skye last week and we buried them yesterday. Their fishing boat was found up near Applecross three weeks ago, unmanned and the engine out of fuel. Poor Maggie and Seonaid, lucky for them the bairns are full grown and off their hands now.

Lachie Just-The-One-Then was at the sheep fank tool store by midday, where he fired up the stove. Poor Lachie, the drink has gripped him since he went away to university. The first Easter holidays he was back and never went away again. Every now and then he tries to shake it off and this was one of these times.

I was there by early afternoon and Shimi and his wife Peigi came in soon after. They're the last of the folk in Achnabeg to be native speakers of the old language and are patient with those who attempt to learn it.

Later on, Helen the blow-in came in. She was sleeping in the back of a wreck of an estate car down by the harbour until Angus Dubh offered her the use of his caravan. It's not good to speak ill of the dead, but Angus wasn't famous for his generosity, so all that's a mystery. I wonder will Maggie Dubh let her stay on?

Anyway, that afternoon we were all huddled round the stove which was red-hot. You know don't you, there's a veil between us and that other world, the one which is full of mischief and spite? But on that day, with the fog rolling in from the sea and people mindful of the funeral, the veil was paper-thin. We're awful modern in Achnabeg with the electric coming thirty years ago and the TV mast on the mainland bringing the wide world to our kitchens, but we're still wary of the *Bean Sidhe*, and any ancestors who might want to hang around, instead of buggering off like decent souls.

Calum Ban had delivered the eulogy at the funeral, and, you have to hand it to him, he did Angus and John-Norman proud. Anyone would think they were the finest, most popular, upstanding men in Achnabeg, instead of... Well, anyway, having turned on the tap, Calum was still in the mood to talk.

'Does anyone here remember young Duncan MacGregor?'

Shimi said, 'It's true that I remember. He was the child who went missing on Christmas day, did he not?' Shimi doesn't really mind the lack of Gaelic among us because he likes to show off his mastery of English.

'How terrible for the parents,' said Helen. She was holding the coffee flask Peigi had brought. It was well laced with whisky, so, before saying anything else, she placed it carefully back on the table far away from Lachie Just-The-One-Then. 'Was he ever found?'

'He was found right enough,' said Calum. 'But not until the spring after. Ach, searches were made, for a light was seen wandering round the top of the moor just a week later, on Hogmanay night. The lad was only twelve, but a strange one. He liked to roam by himself up on the moor all day and did he not take a little torch which he sometimes used on returning home late? All that winter the light was seen, not every night, but enough that his parents, poor Alec and Morag, were nearly driven out of their wits.'

Calum slowed down then. I'd heard the story before and knew what was coming, but last time he'd told it there hadn't been a recent death. He must have weighed it up and decided there was no one there to offend, but sometimes I wonder about Calum Ban. Is he deeper than he lets on?

'Finally they went to old Flora MacKinnon, the *cailleach phiseogach.* Aye, there was always something knowing about Flora. Women went to her to find out who their future husband would be, how many children they would have, who had put the evil eye on their cow to make it swell up – that sort of thing.'

Calum knows how to tell a good story. He paused to open the door of the stove and then threw in a couple of lumps of peat, and we all watched as the flames rose up to consume them. Then he continued.

'When Alec and Morag went to see her about their boy, Flora asked them to come back with something he used to wear. They gave her an old pullover which she held in front of her while closing her eyes. When she opened them again all she could say was: "he sleeps under a white roof". Now Alec and Morag didn't know what to make of that at all, but then someone remembered a time he'd seen the lad skating on the High Loch. Of course there was nothing to do then but to drag the loch. Well do I remember the men hauling the boat up the old cart road, and the chains jingling in its bow. With my own eyes I saw them launching it and throwing the hooks and chains in the water. They were not long at their task. The lad must have fallen through the ice and no one there to help, you see. Well, his remains are buried up there in the Free Church graveyard.'

Calum looked round at everyone. 'The light on the moor was never seen again.'

The wind was shrieking like a *Bean Sidhe* round the fank walls by now, and folk drew closer to the stove. After a while, Shimi got up, opened the door and peered out. 'Blacker it is, than the Earl of Hell's waistcoat,' he said, 'I'm for home, and so too should the rest of you!'

There are days in Achnabeg when I look back on the road I've travelled and see that much of the journey is over. There are nights when a glory morning seems awful far away.

The Blow-In

("The Blow-in" was first published in 2020 in *The Phare*. Editors Steven John and Claire Harrison.)

Helen turned over in her sleeping bag and tried to get comfortable, but her fur hat fell from her head, and then rolled under the front seat of the estate car. Little shafts of sunlight crept around the cardboard she had taped to the windows. She shivered. It was cold, even for a morning in April. A memory of her husband bringing a mug of coffee to her bedside was pushed away.

The seagulls began their hoarse chorus, and one or two thumped onto the roof of the car. The tide was too far out for her to hear the ocean's surge. She thought then she had better be quick, before the local families arrived with their whelk sacks, their children silently fanning out across the beach.

She recalled a day almost a quarter of a century ago, watching her own child running into the sea with wild cries. A smile had arisen and she had turned to share the moment with her husband who, book in hand, read on without looking up.

Six months had passed since she sat outside the school in her car, unable to open the door. She howled out her pain and sorrow in snot-flown tears for an hour, before driving home. The car keys were left beside an apologetic note on the kitchen table. It had seemed fatuous to attempt a continued existence, but she was drawn to the North. She had last visited the highland village of Achnabeg when she was twenty, staying in a canvas ridge tent which was old even then. It was to that time of hope and to that girl she wanted to bid farewell. She had never camped since, but through all the relocations in her life she had hung onto the tent. Sitting beside it in a taxi on her way to the bus station, she'd imagined a couple of days camping by the shore and then a lonely climb to somewhere remote and high, where in time the cold would do its bitter work.

When she got off the bus in Ullapool, she'd hoped to get a lift to Achnabeg in the Post Office Land Rover, but it was in the garage for repairs. After a few minutes thought, she lifted her rucksack onto her back and dragged the heavy old tent to an ironmonger on the main street. There she bought a wheelbarrow. The only one left was red, but colour was of no account in a world reduced to sepia tones. As an afterthought, she bought a cheap pair of climbing boots. Cinching the rucksack straps more firmly round her chest and waist, she dumped the tent in the wheelbarrow and pointed it towards the track which twisted along the coast to Achnabeg.

Six hours later, the first houses came in sight as she trundled the wheelbarrow round the western buttress of Sgùrr nan Spor. She paused, then set the wheelbarrow down and sat on it watching the Atlantic rollers sweep into the bay from the red skies to the west.

After a while, she noticed some rough ground beyond the harbour where a camp could be set up, so she took the wheelbarrow's handles once more. She was tired and her feet seemed to seek out every rock or pothole in her path. The wind strengthened and a light rain began to fall. Not the best conditions for erecting a tent.

At the landward entrance to the harbour someone had left an old estate car; the back axle was propped up on concrete blocks and the remaining tyres were deflated. She trudged past it and then stopped. Looking around, there was no one to be seen, so without much hope she tried the handle of its rear door. It swung up and she looked inside. The rear seats had gone, and in their place were piled-up fishing nets of different colours, green, blue and orange. She pushed them to one side, pulled her sleeping bag from her rucksack and threw it in, stowing the tent and rucksack under the car. The door closed behind her with a satisfying thump and then she passed out.

She woke the following morning to a gentle knock on her window. A chipped mug of piping hot tea was passed in and, as she drank, she viewed the burly rear of the fisherman who had returned to load his boat with creels. That was Calum Ban, good with animals; kind and incurious with human flotsam.

'I'll be needing a hand later on with these creels. Would five pounds be acceptable to you?' Calum had returned for his mug and barely paused to receive his answer. It seemed the fisherman was relying on her, so Helen passed the afternoon exploring the area while she waited for the boat's return. Then she helped transfer the prawns into their lonely test-tube beds, ready for the refrigerated lorry. When the work was finished, Calum Ban removed his nets from the car, waving off her protests, and helped her with erecting the tent. Some days later

Calum showed up with a pair of wheels for the car which allowed them to push it along the strand, away from the bustle of the harbour.

Since then, Helen felt that she had slipped into the slow rhythm of Achnabeg life without it missing a beat. There was the small matter of Peadar the Fiddle, who from his caravan window had watched her progress with her red wheelbarrow from the minute she came round Sgùrr nan Spor. He had sat down that night to compose a tune to the mystery woman. Later on, he called it 'Helen MacFarlane's March to Achnabeg', but if Peadar, immortalising her in such a fashion, had hopes of trespassing beyond the troubled gaze of Helen MacFarlane's green eyes, his hopes were doomed.

She helped Calum and the other fishermen with odd jobs, and she ranged along the coast picking whelks from the rock pools where they liked to gather. She was content with solitude, and the rest of Achnabeg respected that, but most evenings the local kids swarmed round the car. They teased out her past with the deftness of prosecution lawyers. Taking it in turns to throw questions at her, they cross-examined where it was obvious she was leading them up a blind alley.

'OK, you've got me. NASA didn't sack me because of my fear of heights. Actually, I wasn't even an astronaut.'

This was met with groans, some of satisfaction, lamentations from others.

'I mean, being a bullfighter in Spain hardly fits you to work for NASA, does it?'

A chorus of supplementary questions.

'Yes, yes, I loved that job.' She gestured with her hands as if wielding a cape. 'But I loved my boyfriend more. He turned vegetarian.'

In the end they all agreed she was doing secret work for the Navy base in Kyle and Helen was satisfied with that.

One evening she went for a ramble along the shore. The path veered away from the beach to the top of a hill. As Helen climbed higher, she heard the reedy sound of a highland chanter being played. On the other side of the hill, in a clearing of birch and alder, stood a caravan, discoloured and dented in places, with a rusted iron chimney sticking out through the roof. On its steps sat a girl she hadn't seen before, barely into her teens, brown hair falling forward over her face as she played a slow air. Helen closed her eyes. She had shut the door to sadness, but her attention was pulled in by the tune's melancholy air which seemed to whisper,

No more, no more, no more forever, farewell, farewell, farewell

After a while Helen could take no more and crept away.

A few minutes later, as she strode along the track, a voice from behind said, 'Did ye no like ma playin' then?'

Helen wheeled round. It was the girl. Brown hair now tied back loosely with a rag, her face swarthy, a knowing look in her brown eyes. She was clad in a man's brown wool jumper which was caught up by a thick leather belt at the waist, the rest hanging to mid-thigh, sleeves rolled up to her elbows. Cheap blue jeans were rolled up to reveal black plimsolls.

'I liked it fine,' she said, and turned back to the path.

The girl chuckled and fell in beside her. 'Well, I'll play for ye again no doubt. That is if ye're here to stay?'

Helen gave her a puzzled look.

'Are ye not a blow-in like us? Me and mam just arrived last week and I dinnae ken if we'll stay.'

Helen understood now, but was surprised. The girl's weather-beaten skin and natural confidence seemed so much of a piece with the raw character of the west coast that she had thought her a local.

'So,' said Meg. 'Ye know where I live now, so mebbe I'll take a gander at your place.'

'I wasn't...' Helen realised there was no point in arguing.

'You're welcome...em...what's your name?'

'What's yours?'

'Helen MacFarlane. Pleased to meet you.'

The girl's eyes took in Helen's hand, which was held out to her.

'Meg,' she said, walking on.

When they got to the car, they paused as Meg took in the small ridge tent beside it, the brown canvas walls filling out and relaxing with each eddy of the wind.

'Oh,' said Meg. She looked from the camp to Helen. 'Are ye one of the Brora MacFarlanes then?'

'No, I'm from Edinburgh.' Helen smiled as she realised the misunderstanding. 'I've never lived in a tent before.'

'I can see that,' said Meg. 'I thought ye were from the Brora crowd. My granma said they're no dainty either.'

'Do you live with your granny, then?'

'Naw, I live with my mam. Granma's deid.' Meg's features softened then.

'I'm sorry to hear that. Is it just the two of you?'

'Aye,' said Meg, suddenly watchful.

I won't ask about her father.

'Is your grandfather still alive?'

'Who knows, maybe,' said Meg. She picked up a stone and threw it into the sea. 'Grandpa disappeared after the war. Granma never got over it.'

'Oh,' said Helen, 'he might still be alive, then?'

The girl looked at her with suspicion.

I've gone too far.

'Oh, he might be, right enough,' Meg said, and turned to go. 'I'm gonna nash. Mam will have made the tea.' Then she jerked her thumb back at Helen's tent. 'Remind me to give ye some tips, if ye're stayin'.' With that she was off, back along the track.

Well, she's a salty wee thing, thought Helen, but, inside, it was as if a tiny candle flame had sprung to life. That evening, as Helen sat adding driftwood to the campfire she had built on the shore, she found herself wondering if Meg meant what she said about helping her with the tent. For the time being, the car would have to do.

One day while she was distracted by a sea-eagle wheeling around the peak of Sgùrr nan Spor, inevitably it was Meg who extracted more information than Helen was quite ready to share.

'How many kids d'ye have?' she had murmured, her dark-brown eyes shifting away from Helen as she spoke.

Helen had replied without thinking. 'Only one...' And then she caught herself. 'Yes, just one.'

Now, she released the catch on the rear door, allowing it to swing up to reveal the morning. She got out and moved around the car to inspect herself in the wing mirror. Calum Ban had allowed her to use his shower the day before. She pushed her hair back from her face and frowned at the crows' feet in the corners of her eyes and the faint wrinkles at the sides of her mouth. A smile usually got rid of them and she tried one now, revealing teeth not quite as white as she would like. *For god's sake, I'm forty-five.*

She busied herself with her camp stove and soon had the blackened kettle singing its old song. Perched on the rear of the estate, sleeping bag wrapped around her shoulders and hugging her coffee cup to her chest, Helen watched the seas heaving against the rocks in the bay. The tide had turned and it was time to go whelk-picking.